The Boy Who Lived In Pudding Lane

the Boy
Who Lived In
Pudding Lane

Being a True Account, if only you believe
it, of the Life and Ways of Santa,
Oldest Son of Mr. and Mrs. Claus

by SARAH ADDINGTON

Illustrated by
GERTRUDE A. KAY

Grafton & Scratch
PUBLISHERS

Pᴘʀᴇꜰᴀᴄᴇ

THIS BRIEF BIOGRAPHY *of a great hero, Santa Claus, is entered upon with the reverence due to the nature of the undertaking, and with the timidity that necessarily arises from the fact that it is a breaking of new ground.*

Just why historians have, in all epic accounts, ignored probably the greatest international figure that ever existed, is a mystery to the author, for whom the antecedents, early life, and young manhood of Santa Claus have always been immensely fascinating. Nevertheless, the life of this great man has never been written; and even Mr. Wells, in a history of life from the amœba to the Peace Conference, has not so much as a footnote on Santa Claus, though there are critics of youthful, and therefore unprejudiced, minds, who will rate him far above Napoleon, Lincoln, and Garibaldi.

To shed light, then, on the life of a popular idol, shamefully neglected by historians, is the purpose of this little study, which has been carefully and scientifically compiled from original sources.

The author is fully aware that her book cannot add a single huzza to the world's acclaim of Santa Claus (for he has gloriously risen above the conspiracy of historians to world-wide celebrity). She writes the account to please herself, and possibly a few other fellow admirers (preferably under twelve), who, like her, must know where Santa Claus lived as a little boy, what his mother was like, and how he got started in his enchanting business, before admitting this to be a perfect world.

S.A.

CONTENTS

The little boy who lived in Pudding Lane was always dressed in a bright red suit

The Boy Who Lived In Pudding Lane

INTRODUCING THE FAMILY

ONCE UPON A TIME, in the kingdom of Old King Cole, there lived a father and a mother, and a fat little boy who was always dressed in a bright red suit. The father, whose name was Mr. Claus, was a baker, and he lived in Pudding Lane, between the butcher and the candle-stick-maker.

Mr. Claus was really about the best baker in the world. He knew so well how to make little cake puppies, with red-currant eyes. And he knew so well how to make funny gingerbread Brownies, with black-raisin eyes. He made great fat loaves of bread, warm and golden and crusty. And he made little plum tarts, that a boy could eat up in one gobble, and a girl could eat up in two.

All the boys and girls who lived in Pudding Lane used to play around Mr. Claus's shop, and Mr. Claus, being a generous baker, almost always gave them cake-dough puppies, or gingerbread Brownies, when they came. And often, when he was busy, he would send out his little boy, Santa, to give the children their pastries.

The children loved the little fat Santa even more than they did the cake-dough puppies and the gingerbread Brownies. He was such a jolly little chap, with a smile that crinkled up his round nose, blue eyes brimful of merriment, and a waddle that made all the children laugh, as he staggered under loaves and cookies.

"You look like your grandmother's gander when you walk," they would cry.

And sure enough, he did walk very much like his grandmother's gander. But this was a high honor, indeed, for his Grandmother was that great person, Mother Goose, and her gander was a bird much admired by the children of Pudding Lane.

Almost every day the children would come, and Santa would give them sweet things from the bakeshop until they couldn't eat any more. Pretty soon, Mr. Claus began to complain.

"How can I make money, Santa, if you give away everything and leave me nothing to sell? Yesterday, you gave away every cookie in the shop, and left only the cinnamon cow on the counter. And her right horn was broken off."

But little Santa knew that his father was not serious, and that everything was really going very well indeed. For they were warm and cosy in their rooms behind the shop, and they had plenty of hot soup and sausages to eat. Moreover, every night, when the butcher and the candlestick-maker came over to sit with the baker, they always said that business was good, and praised Old King Cole to the skies.

Santa would give them sweet things from the bake-shop until they couldn't eat any more

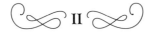

SANTA'S BROTHERS COME TO TOWN

THEN, ONE DAY, Santa was told that he had two little brothers.

"Two!" he cried.

This *was* a surprise. And sure enough, there in the cradle near the stove, he saw them, a pair of squirming, purplish objects, who made dreadful faces at him when he peeped at them, and who gave out strange noises. They were very odd creatures, indeed, and little Santa wondered if they'd ever grow up to be anything at all, with that start.

But they did. They soon learned to smile, in a wide, toothless fashion that made Santa laugh uproariously. Then they astonished him by walking. Little Santa began to see that they were turning into human beings, after all. And just as he was beginning to like the little fellows very much indeed, he was told, one morning, that two more little brothers had come to town.

Two more! This was astounding. Santa could hardly believe his ears. And yet, when he went to look, there they were, two more little squirming, purplish things in the same old cradle.

The butcher and the candlestick-maker came over to pay their respects. The butcher brought a juicy chop for the mother of the five little Claus boys, and the candlestick-maker brought a lovely pewter candleholder. But Mr. Claus appeared very doleful.

"I don't see how I can feed so many," he confided to his friends.

"Cheer up, they're all boys, and they'll be earning their own bread before you know it," said the candlestick-maker consolingly.

"Yes, cheer up," said the butcher.

"There's Santa, now, almost six. I'll give him a job as an errand-boy before many months."

Mr. Claus shook his head sadly.

"He'd give away all your chops and chickens, as he gives away my cookies and tarts now."

Santa heard this and, for the first time since he was a baby, he wanted to cry. He felt so sorry for his father! His poor father, who worked night and day, and seemed so to be so worried. Little Santa made up his mind then and there to stop giving pastries away so profusely.

MOTHER GOOSE COMES TO VISIT

THAT AFTERNOON, Santa lay on the ground, watching the clouds roll by. There were great puffy clouds, that made him think of the wool on Bo-Peep's flock. There were little stringy clouds, like the rags in Mrs. Claus's rag-bag. There were slim silver clouds, that swam around like fishes in the blue ocean of the sky. And there was one beautiful peaked cloud, that looked like a snow-covered mountain.

Santa, on his back, watched the clouds a long time, thinking gravely of his hard-working father. Finally he grew sleepy, and he had almost dozed off, when suddenly, over the top of the beautiful peaked cloud, he saw a black speck appear.

"It must be a bird," said Santa to himself.

The speck came nearer and grew larger and blacker; and then, all at once, Santa jumped to his feet, and began waving frantically. For the speck was a great deal more than a bird. It was Santa's grandmother, old Mother Goose, coming to visit them on her highflying gander.

In just a minute, there she was on the ground beside him, twinkling eyes, sharp nose, pointed hat, and all. At the sight of her, all the children came running; and as for Santa, well, he just jumped up and down with excitement and joy.

Mother Goose smiled at them all, gave Santa a good grandmotherly hug, took off her glasses and wiped them, shook some strawberry lollypops out of her pockets, and then rushed into the house. For, of course, Mother Goose was more interested in her daughter, Mrs. Claus, and her new

In just a minute, there she was on the ground beside him

grandsons, than she was in the village children.

Everything seemed more cheerful after Mother Goose got there.

"It's nice to have a lot of children," she told the melancholy Mr. Claus. "Look at the Old Woman Who Lives in a Shoe. She has so many children she doesn't know what to do. But she wouldn't know what to do if she *didn't* have them, because she told me so. And it's a good thing for little Santa that he has brothers," she went on, "or he would have been spoiled. There's Mistress Mary, an only child, and such a contrary girl I never saw. If she had little brothers and sisters to think about, she'd soon get over that contrariness."

"But she has a very pretty garden," put in Santa.

For every day he stopped to look at Mistress Mary's garden, which was right next to the pasture where the Claus's cow fed.

"Fiddlesticks!" said Mother Goose, "Silver bells and cockle-shells! Who wants to raise such useless nothings? That girl ought to be growing cabbages and corn."

Mother Goose was a very practical old lady, you see. But although little Santa liked cabbage-soup and corn-bread as well as anybody, he secretly was glad that Mistress Mary had a beautiful, and not a useful, garden. For, when the wind blew, he could almost hear the silver bells ring in the garden. And when the sun shone, the cockle-shells glistened as brightly as they did on the seashore where they came from.

At supper, around the hearthstone, the family gossiped comfortably of this and that.

"Simple Simon says he met you going to the fair," said Mother Goose to Mr. Claus, helping herself to another jelly bun.

"Yes, I took some pies to the fair," replied Mr. Claus, "and Simon asked me to let him taste my ware. But the fellow didn't have a penny, so I couldn't give him any, of course."

Mr. Claus took another bowlful of soup from the pot on the hearth.

"Well, Simon is a real simpleton," said Mother Goose, "but he's a harmless fellow. My goodness, Santa child, no wonder you're a roly-poly puddin' and pie! That's the third helping of porridge you've had. He needs a new suit, Nellie." (Nellie was Mrs. Claus's first name.)

"Yes, he does," replied Mrs. Claus. "But I've been so busy making clothes for the other children, I haven't had time for Santa."

"Well, the little fellows look real well in their apple-green trousers and canary-colored coats; but I'm not sure, Nellie, that those suits are as practical as Santa's red ones."

There she was again, just as sensible a grandmother as anybody ever had.

SANTA HAS A SECRET ALL BY HIMSELF

LITTLE SANTA really did stop giving away all his father's pastries. For now that he had four little brothers, he found that he was very busy helping his mother to care for them. And since they were always wanting something, he didn't miss the fun of giving, after all.

If you had four little brothers, you would know just how much there was for Santa to do. He used to feed the first batch of twins (Mr. Claus always spoke of them as "batches," just as if they were cookies). He helped them into their apple-green trousers, and played bear with them in the backyard. He held the second batch, one on each knee, while they drank milk from pewter mugs, and crunched crackers between their new little teeth.

But although the little Claus babies were warm and well fed and rosy, they didn't have any toys to play with, like a good many other children in Pudding Lane. And little Santa, who was now seven years old, going on eight, used to worry a great deal about that. For he could see how much fun the other children had with their hobbyhorses and kites and blocks.

Then it was that Santa had a wonderful idea. It was really the most wonderful idea a little boy ever had. It was a great secret, too, and he didn't tell anybody, not even his mother. But his mother knew that he had a secret, for he would go to the wood-shed and stay there sometimes all after-noon, and she could hear the sound of hammering and sawing. And one day, when Santa came in to supper after a long afternoon in the woodshed, his father sniffed the air and said:—

"I smell red paint."

Little Santa gave a jump and asked:—

"How can you tell it's red by smelling it?"

"Oh," said Mr. Claus," can't I tell white icing from chocolate, when I smell it? Then why can't I tell red paint from yellow with the same nose?"

Santa pondered this deeply. He really didn't see where his father was wrong, and yet *he* couldn't tell the color of paint from its smell, no matter how hard he sniffed. He kept on wondering about it until he went to bed, when he found that red paint came off on his washcloth from his left cheek. Then he knew that his father had been teasing him, and he chuckled aloud at the joke.

But still little Santa did not tell where the red paint came from, and nobody asked any questions. He kept on going out to the woodshed every day, and all the time his secret kept getting more wonderful. Santa even dreamed about it at night; and in the morning, when he jumped out of bed, it was the first thing he thought of.

SANTA ALMOST TELLS
THE WONDERFUL SECRET

IT WAS GETTING pretty cold these days. Mother Goose had dived deep into the walnut chest and brought out all the family woolens. Father Claus had stuffed the wood-box full of hickory logs.

Almost every night Jack Frost came while the family were all asleep, and, with a silver needle, he embroidered the cottage windows, left shining roses patterned there, lacy spider webs, and a thousand stars or two. Santa used to try to catch Jack Frost at his work, but he never, never could.

It was cold in the woodshed, too; but Santa kept going there; and every night, when he came back for supper, his cheeks were redder than ever, and his fat little hands looked like purple plums.

"It'll be the Holy Day next week," observed his mother one night at table. "We must get a new candlestick from the candlestick-maker, and a fine goose from the butcher, and we will all sing carols the night before, in honor of the Holy Child's birthday."

When Mrs. Claus mentioned the Holy Child's birthday, little Santa almost wriggled out of his chair, and he honestly thought for a moment that his wonderful secret was going to burst right out from his lips. So he buttoned them together more tightly than ever, until his jaws fairly ached with the effort.

Mrs. Claus noticed his ill-concealed excitement.

"My goodness, Santa, what are you wriggling all over your chair about? Sit up straight there, like a good boy. It's only a baby that may squirm like that."

MRS. CLAUS GETS READY
FOR THE HOLY DAY

M RS. CLAUS soon began to prepare for the Holy Day. First, she went to the candlestick-maker next door and asked to see his new stock.

The candlestick-maker was a little, thin, bent-over man, with a face like a fox. Many people thought him objectionable, and it is true that he was forever making his nephew Jack jump over a candlestick, which was rather an unpleasant habit. Jack was nimble, and Jack was quick, and did not really seem to mind very much.

Still, most of the villagers thought the candlestick-maker very disagreeable to keep Jack jumping that way all the time.

However, the Clauses liked the candle-stick-maker very much, and he liked them.

When Mrs. Claus went into the shop, the candlestick-maker jumped up from his work-bench, smoothed out his dirty leather apron, and smiled his best smile. He didn't have a tooth in his head, poor man, so his smile was rather queer until you got used to it.

Mrs. Claus looked over the new stock of candlesticks, pewter and brass and copper. And they were all so beautiful, the poor lady could not, for the life of her, decide which one she wanted. For the pewter one had a handle as delicately turned as a bracelet. The brass one had been polished until it glittered like a sunbeam in the candlestick-maker's old, dark shop. And the copper one was tall and red like a tiger lily.

Well, Mrs. Claus just stood and looked

at them all, until her eyes ached. Finally, she gave it up.

"Tell me, neighbor, which one I shall choose," she besought the candlestick-maker.

The old man smiled, and laid the copper holder in her hand.

Then Mrs. Claus declared that it was the very one she had wanted all the time.

"Then why didn't you pick it out yourself?" asked the curious Santa.

The old candlestick-maker cackled and showed his toothless gums.

"The little fellow don't know women do he?" he asked Mrs. Claus

Mrs. Claus laughed, too; and just then, Jack, the candlestick-maker's nephew, came into the shop.

The candlestick-maker turned a sharp face to his nephew.

"Jack, be nimble, Jack, be quick—" he began. But Mrs. Claus did not care to stay for the exhibition, and hastily left the shop.

They next went to the butcher's, on the other side of their own house.

"Ho, ho, ho!" said the butcher, when he saw them coming, "here's company. Sorry I can't offer you a pipe, Mrs. Claus, but something tells me you wouldn't accept it if I did, ho, ho, ho!"

The butcher was, you see, a very genial person. His jokes were not always good jokes, to be sure. But as Mrs. Claus said, a jokester can't always turn out a funny joke, any more than a baker can, every single time, turn out a perfect pie. She said this one time to Mr. Claus, when he grumbled that the butcher's jests were sometimes tiresome.

The butcher was a big, broad-chested fellow, with great arms, fine yellow moustaches, and an enormous white apron that covered him from chin to toe. And Mrs. Claus always said that he had the best meat in the kingdom. How Mrs. Claus knew this was something of a mystery, for she had never been outside the town, and there was no other butcher in Pudding Lane. Still, Mrs. Claus always said this, and nobody questioned her word. And by-and-by, everybody in Pudding Lane began to say that this butcher had the best meat in the kingdom, though not one of them had ever tasted any other meat.

Today Mrs. Claus bought a handful of tripe, and then she asked the butcher: "What about your Holy Day fowl?"

"Finest in the kingdom, Mrs. Claus," replied the butcher, rubbing his hands together.

At last Santa understood. His mother had learned that this meat was the best in the kingdom because the butcher said so himself! And, of course, he knew.

So Mrs. Claus ordered a gray goose for the Holy Day, and they departed.

"Gray geese are good eating, Santa," she told the little boy on the way home, "and gray-goose feathers don't get so dirty in bed pillows."

When they got home, Mrs. Claus declared that they must all get down to business immediately and learn their Holy Day carols. So she got out a kitchen spoon to beat time with, and they all got down to business and sang carols. Father Claus rumbled and roared. Mother Claus sang high and loud, and got very red in the face. Santa shouted his best, now in the soprano part, now in the alto, and often halfway between. The first batch of twins yelled fervently on one note. And the babies squealed with delight at the racket. When they had all sung until they were hoarse and breathless, Mother Claus laid down the spoon.

"Now we're all ready for the Holy Child's birthday," she said.

And once more, little Santa nearly burst with his wonderful secret, which he had kept so many days.

THE WONDERFUL SECRET COMES OUT

THE DAY before the Holy Child's birthday, Mrs. Claus couldn't find Santa, high or low. He wasn't in the butcher's or the candlestick-maker's. He wasn't in the woodshed. He wasn't anywhere. Mrs. Claus got very impatient.

"Here I am, cooking a goose, making new candles, scrubbing the hearth, and there's no Santa to help me do a thing," she said to Mr. Claus at dinner. "Where in the kingdom do you suppose the child is?"

But Mr. Claus didn't know. So Mrs. Claus had to go on with her work without any help from anybody. She certainly was very annoyed, and was preparing to give Santa a good scolding when he got back.

He had never done such a naughty think before. In fact, he had never done anything really naughty before, and Mrs. Claus didn't know what to make of him.

But it grew dark, and Santa didn't come back; and then Mrs. Claus got fearfully worried. She put on a hood and went hurrying down Pudding Lane to the Town Crier's.

"Get out your bell, Mr. Crier," she said.

"What, is pussy in the well again?" asked the Crier.

"Worse than that," replied Mrs. Claus. "My oldest boy, Santa, is lost."

"Have you looked upstairs and downstairs and in my lady's chamber?" asked the Town Crier.

"We have no upstairs and we have no lady's chamber," answered Mrs. Claus; "but we have searched every nook of the downstairs, and he hasn't been home for hours upon hours, and now it's as black as a witch outdoors."

So the Town Crier left his supper and took out his great bronze bell. He went up and down Pudding Lane. He went east to the crossroads and west to the bridge. He went up and down Pinafore Pike and down and up Raspberry Road. And everywhere he sang out: "Little Santa Claus is lost! All folks turn out and hunt!"

And as the Crier went his round, Mr. and Mrs. Claus sat beside the stove, each one hugging a batch of twins, mourning their lost boy, the jolly, fat, good little Santa.

"The fire in the hearth is out," said Mrs. Claus to her husband.

"The fire in my heart is out, too," said Mr. Claus.

"We haven't lighted the Holy Child's candle," replied Mrs. Claus. "Let us put it in the window so our own child may see it and come home."

So they waited, weeping and sad, the little brothers asleep in their arms, while the men of the neighborhood gathered lanterns and ropes and bells, and started out to find the lost child.

It was quiet and cold in the little room back of the shop. No sound came out to the waiting mother and father. The Holy Child's candle winked and blinked in the window. What a sad Holy Day for the Claus family!

Then suddenly, with a bump and a clatter, down the chimney came a red-clad figure, with a bag on his arm and a merry chuckle.

"Why, Santa Claus!" exclaimed his mother, jumping up to hug her little boy.

Father Claus jumped up, too, and the four little brothers woke up and immediately began to laugh at the sight of their roly-poly Santa, who had a smudge on his cheek and was dancing and laughing as if he would split his fat little sides.

"Santa Claus," cried Mrs. Claus, again, "wherever have you been?"

And then came the wonderful secret.

"I have toys for my little brothers," cried Santa. "I kept them in a box on the roof, so, of course, I had to come down the chimney. Good thing I'm fat, mother, or it would have scraped my bones."

He laughed again and began to open his bag. And his brothers' eyes got as big as moons at the things he tumbled out!

"Here's a rocking horse for Matthew," he shouted, "and a kite for little Mark. Here's a set of blocks for Luke, and a top that spins for John!"

Such hilarity as there was then! Matthew climbed on the wooden horse and rocked

'I have toys for my little brothers,' cried Santa

until he was dizzy and fell over backwards on his head. It was a peculiar-looking horse, made of boards and barrel-staves, with its green yarn tail stuck 'way on the right side by mistake. But it did rock, oh my, yes! Little Santa had spent days balancing it on its barrel-stave rockers.

Mark shouted with glee over his blue paper kite. Luke build a high tower of blocks that tumbled right over on John's whirling top. And everybody danced and screamed at everything that happened.

HONORS FOR SANTA

FINALLY, when they were all out of breath, Mother Claus brought in cinnamon eggnog, and Father Claus built up the fire.

"Santa, however did you think of such a beautiful surprise?" asked Mother Claus.

Little Santa almost fell out of his chair with delight. But he couldn't give his mother any satisfactory answer.

"I just did," was all that he could say.

"And how did you learn to make those toys out of kindling wood and left-over bits?" asked his father.

"I don't know," he answered, blushing with pride and pleasure at his father's question.

"Won't the neighbors all be surprised when they hear of this?" asked Mrs. Claus.

And then she remembered something and gave a little cry.

"My goodness, Mr. Claus," she said to her husband, "do you suppose the men are still out looking for Santa? We were so excited about the toys we forgot to tell them he was found again."

"Great snakes!" exclaimed Mr. Claus. ("Great snakes!" was his favorite expression, but if the poor man had ever seen a great snake, I'm sure he would have run many miles.)

He jumped up to run and tell the Crier, but just then all the men who had been hunting for little Santa, came up Pudding Lane to the door.

"We can't find him," said the leader of the search-party. Then he looked in through the door and saw all the Clauses, merry as could be, around the blazing fire, with Santa in their midst.

"What's this?" he asked frowning. "Did you play a hoax on us, baker?"

All the men began to growl, and for a moment it sounded like a storm coming up a mile away.

Mr. Claus quickly began to explain.

"It was a Holy Day surprise," he said. "Little Santa made all these toys for this brothers, and came down the chimney with them. We thought he was lost, but he was only on the roof."

"I would have come sooner, only I went to sleep," confessed Santa.

"Come in, friends," urged Mr. Claus, "and look at the things our Santa made. He'll make a first-rate apprentice, Mr. Carpenter."

So all the men came in, and looked at the things Santa had made.

"First-class," said the carpenter, rocking

the horse. He didn't seem to notice that the green year tail was not in the centre.

"This top really spins," said the candle-stick-maker, on his knees.

"I wish Jack had some blocks like this," said Mr. Horner. It was a well known fact that every Holy Day Jack sat in the corner, pulling plums out of his pie, and telling everybody what a smart boy he was. Which was very tiresome, of course.

So it was that Santa found himself much admired and complimented. Finally, however, after all the men had drunk eggnog, wiped off their moustaches carefully, and departed for home, Santa went to bed. And he knew that his wonderful secret had been a huge success, and he resolved to make toys for his little brothers every single Holy Day.

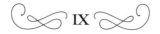

BAD NEWS FROM HAMELIN

IT WAS SHORTLY after Holy Day that the Clauses brought out the old cradle for a new baby, and this time it was a girl! How pleased everybody was! Nobody felt doleful this time, for Mr. Claus had learned that the soup always did go round, after all. And Mother Claus had wished so hard for a daughter.

The baby girl grew fast as the spring came along; and by summer, when the winds were warm and the bushes on Raspberry Road showed little green knobs, she began to be fretful.

"Her teeth ache," said the piper's wife, as she held her one day.

"Her teeth?" exclaimed Santa. "How could they ache? She hasn't any!"

Santa laughed aloud at the blunder the piper's wife had made.

"Of course, she has teeth," replied the piper's wife promptly, "only you can't see 'em, Santa. Ha, ha, the joke's on you." Little Santa, feeling rather foolish, said no more.

Mrs. Claus came out of the house with her sewing. And as Santa sat drowsily in the sun, watching the bees and dragon-flies and humming-birds in their flight from flower to flower, the two women chatted.

"And, where's the baker today?" asked the piper's wife. "I noticed the shop was closed."

"He's gone to the royal kitchen to teach the Queen of Hearts how to make her favorite tarts," answered Mrs. Claus proudly.

She was so glad the piper's wife had asked the question. For the Clauses had thought it a great honor for the Queen of Hearts to send for the baker, and Mrs. Claus *did* want everybody to know of the occasion.

The piper's wife had a piece of news from Hamelin.

"They say there's a plaque of rats over there," she said.

"My goodness!" said Mrs. Claus. "Are they very bad?"

"Very bad," replied the piper's wife. "They get in the porridge, and climb in the beds, and swarm the streets."

"Dear me!" said Mrs. Claus. "That is terrible."

"Yes," went on the piper's wife, "but there's a piper, —my husband knows him— who has agreed to pipe them all away for a certain sum of money."

"Well, that's a blessing," said Mrs. Claus. "Think of having rats in your babies' beds."

She shivered, and though the day was very warm, little Santa shivered too, at the very thought of rats in his bed.

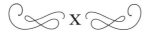

SEVERAL THINGS HAPPEN

M RS. CLAUS WAS going to have a party.
She wrote her invitations with
great pains: "Mrs. Claus humbly craves
the honor of your presence—". And in
the lower left-hand corner, she added:
"Q. E. D."

"What does it mean?" asked the baker.

"I don't know, rightly," replied his wife;
"but they always put it at the bottom of
invitations."

"Well, it ought to have a 'U' in it," criticized
the baker. "'Q' is always followed by 'U.'"

"It does hardly seem right," admitted
Mrs. Claus; but she sent the invitations
that way just the same.

All the grown-ups in Pudding Lane were
invited, and everyone accepted. Mrs. Claus

then began to plan her refreshments. It was a hard problem, for there were Mr. And Mrs. Spratt, who were so queer about meat, and there was Miss Muffet, who was on a diet of curds and whey. Finally, Mrs. Claus decided to have everything she could think of, and then everybody would be pleased.

The day was set for Wednesday, the hour was ten minutes after three, and now, on Tuesday, there was a great cleaning and scrubbing and cooking going on in the little cottage. Santa was a great help. He went up the hill for water, and never stumbled once, though it was the same hill where Jack and Jill had had their frightful accident. He scoured the copper candlestick, which was tall and red, with a tiger lily. He took care of Matthew, Mark, Luke, and John, and his little sister.

In the midst of everything, the butcher came running back into the house, followed by the baker and the candlestick-maker.

"Whatever is the matter?" asked Mrs. Claus. "I don't fancy having three men at their ease in my kitchen whilst I work at a thousand and one things."

"Fetch all the children," commanded the baker. "Fetch Santa and the first batch of twins and the second batch of twins; fetch the little one, and take them all to your breast and hold them there!"

Mrs. Claus stared at her husband. "Has the good man lost his wits, neighbor?" she asked the candlestick-maker.

"Do as he says, Mrs. Claus," replied the candlestick-maker; "and be nimble, be quick!"

Mrs. Claus turned to the butcher.

"Are they stark mad, butcher?" she asked. "Tell me, quick, has the summer heat curdled their brains and addled their minds completely?"

The butcher began to speak.

"First collect your children—"

But Mrs. Claus, poor woman, began to cry, and then they hastened to explain.

"It's that piper from Hamelin," said the baker. "He piped away the rats; but the mayor wouldn't pay, so he's piped away the children into a big, deep pit. And now the Town Crier says he's on his way here—"

Mrs. Claus screamed and ran into the yard. In two minutes she had all her children herded into the kitchen. And in another two minutes, she had them all in one bed, with cotton stuffed in their ears.

"There," she said,"it's precious little piping you'll hear now."

Then she went about her work.

But the children were not so well pleased, and all but Santa, who knew the danger that threatened them, set up a lusty howl.

They cried so hard, that finally Mrs. Claus got some cotton and put it in her own ears.

"There," said she, "let them cry. I can do my work in peace."

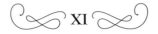

XI

THE DAY OF THE PARTY

THE NEXT MORNING, the Town Crier gave out the news that the Pied Piper of Hamelin had headed the other way. So all the Claus children jumped out of bed, pulled the cotton out of their ears, and rejoiced loudly at their freedom. But this was the Day of the Party, and bustling preparations were soon on foot again.

"Why is the party called for ten minutes after three?" asked Mr. Claus at dinnertime. They were all stuffing their food down hurriedly, in order to get the table cleared before the company should come.

"Well, a body has to set some time or other," answered Mrs. Claus," and ten minutes after three sounded genteel to me."

Mr. Claus did not understand this, and neither did Santa, but Mrs. Claus was well content with the hour.

Oh, such a scramble as it was to get all the Clauses dressed for the party! First Mr. Claus had to have a clean baker's apron and cap, starched so stiff that he scarcely dared move. Then Santa had to scrub his ears, brush his red suit, and shine his shoes until they hurt his eyes with their glare.

After that, the first batch of twins were washed and put into their apple-green trousers and canary colored coats; the next batch were washed and put into their funny little bloomers and shirts of orange and blue.

Good gracious, it was nearly ten minutes after three!

The baby was hurried into her white dress, and at last Mrs. Claus appeared, with her hair curled, her feet in new slippers, and, instead of her old brown apron, she wore a handsome dress of green muslin.

She smiled at Santa, but her smile did not last longer than a second, for she confessed that her new slippers did pinch horribly.

"Whatever made you get'em so small?" asked Mr. Claus. He was fussy and nervous, poor man. Parties didn't come easy to him.

"It was the only pair they had in the shop," said Mrs. Claus. "What else could I do ?"

Then she hobbled to the door on her poor pinched feet, and looked down Pudding Lane.

"Mercy on us, here they come!" she cried, lining up the family in a nice straight row.

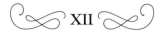

XII

THE PARTY

SURE ENOUGH, down Pudding Lane they came, in their best bibs and tuckers: old Mother Hubbard, Mr. and Mrs. Spratt, Miss Muffet and her mother, Tommy Tucker's parents, the piper and his wife, Dr. Foster, old Toby Sizer, and all the rest. It was indeed, a most imposing procession.

Mrs. Claus shook hands with everybody, hoped they were well, and offered them chairs. They sat in a circle, while Mrs. Claus and Mrs. Claus and Santa hurried to pass around food. For, of course, the food was the main thing.

There were great rolls of freshly browned sausage. There were plates of steaming onions. There was a bite of cheese for everybody. There were fruits, and plenty of pastries from the shop. Miss Muffet had a special bowl of curds and whey, but her mother, bless you, had three helpings of sausage. It had always been said that she thought her daughter's diet a bit silly. Mother Hubbard was seen to slip a bit of meat into her pocket. The old woman always did that at parties. And finally, when all the company had eaten until they could not hold another crumb, there was conversation.

"I notice you limp some, Mrs. Claus. Have a crick in your knee?" asked Mrs. Horner politely.

"No," confessed Mrs. Claus with a slight moan, "I have no crick in my knee, neighbor. But my shoes," —she was ashamed to admit it but she went on bravely,— "my shoes are too tight."

"Why, Mrs. Claus," said Mrs. Horner, reprovingly, "you ought not to wear a tight

They sat in a circle, while Mrs. Claus and Mr. Claus and Santa hurried to pass around food

shoe. Better throw the pair away than ruin good feet."

Old Toby Sizer, the miser, grunted at such extravagance; and Mrs. Spratt who was a very thrifty woman, spoke up.

"Oh, I would never throw them away, Mrs. Claus," she said. "Why don't you save them until your little girl grows up? They would do nicely her when she is a young woman."

This was considered a happy idea by all present, and so Mrs. Claus excused herself and went into the bedroom. When she returned to the company, it was in old house-slippers. It was true that they did not look any too handsome worn with that elegant green muslin dress. But the good lady was comfortable, at any rate.

Just as she joined the party again, a messenger appeared at the door.

"Old King Cole is calling for his fiddlers three," he said. "Are they here, baker?"

Three skinny little men, with fiddles under their arms, sprang forward, wiping the last crumbs from their sharp chins.

"Yes, we are," spoke up the first fiddler. "We'll follow immediately, messenger."

Then, when the messenger had gone, the first fiddler spoke again, this time in a grumbling tone.

"Never go anywhere that that man doesn't send for us," he said.

Mrs. Claus murmured in a consoling manner, and the piper's wife spoke up.

"But he's a merry old soul, fiddler."

"Oh, yes," replied the first fiddler, sighing. "But, if he only were not quite so merry, 't would not be such a dog's life for us. Well, good day, all."

The first fiddler sprang out of the door, and the other fiddlers sprang out after him. The fiddlers three always jumped and leaped everywhere. People said it was because they were so used to jumping for the King.

Little Santa was more sorry than anybody else that they had gone, for he did love a jolly jig such as they played. But his mother had other plans for him anyway, it seemed.

"It is time for the cow, Santa," she reminded him.

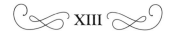

SANTA HAS A WONDERFUL ADVENTURE

SANTA DID NOT like to leave the party, but, of course, he could not neglect the poor cow, either. So out he went, resolved to hurry and get her back before the company should leave. The pasture was at the other end of Pudding Lane, next to Mistress Mary's garden; and Santa hurried there as fast as his legs would carry him.

All at once, he heard a faint noise, like the whistle of a far-away redbird. He looked high above him into all the trees, and he looked low into the bushes, but he saw nothing but green leaves everywhere, no sign of any bird.

The whistling came louder and louder, and then, as Santa got closer to the pasture, he saw Mistress Mary hurrying out of her garden. She ran up Raspberry Road, and when Santa looked to see why she was running so fast, he saw all the village children running, too. And in front of them was a dancing man in brown, piping the most wonderful tune that was ever piped in the world.

It was the Pied Piper of Hamelin!—the wicked man who piped children into a pit and left them there to die!

Little Santa was stiff with horror as he saw the dancing, piping man and remembered his rascally deeds. He was so frightened that he just stood still for a moment, and didn't know what to do.

Then, as the music went on, he suddenly wanted to follow it, too. But he remembered his mother's remedy, and quickly tearing some of the white cotton trimming from his red suit, he stuffed it in his ears.

But he kept thinking: "I must save the children of Pudding Lane from the Pied Piper."

So he ran, as hard as his fat legs would go, to catch up with the procession of children that was trooping away on Raspberry Road. Mistress Mary was at the tail end of the procession. She had been so contrary that she would not follow at first. Santa begged her to come back home.

"You'll be shut up in a big black pit, Mistress Mary," he told her.

But, as usual, she would listen to no one.

Santa then ran a little harder, and caught up with the rest of the children, Tommy Tucker, Little Boy Blue, Johnny Stout, Bo-Peep, Jack Horner, Bob Snooks, Jack and Jill, and all the children of the Old Woman Who Lived in a Shoe.

"Come home," he begged them," or the

Pied Piper will take you to a big black cave, as he did the children of Hamelin."

But the children would not listen, but kept dancing along behind the Piper, never knowing the horrible fate that was in store for them.

"Come back to Pudding Lane," entreated Santa again. "You will all be shut up in the pit and never see your mothers any more."

But the children would not heed him, and kept following the dancing man in brown, who piped such a wonderful tune.

Santa was desperate. What could he do? The children would not listen to his warnings. They would soon be in the Pied Piper's big black pit, and all the mothers in Pudding Lane would cry their eyes out.

Santa wrung his fat hands in despair.

The children would not listen, but kept dancing along behind the piper

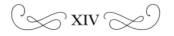

SANTA HAS ANOTHER
MARVELOUS IDEA

*A*ND JUST THEN he had an idea. He shouted to the children again.

"Come home to Pudding Lane, and I will make every one of you a toy for next Holy Day!"

The children turned their backs like a flash on the dancing piper.

"You really will, Santa?" asked Bo-Peep.

"I will," promised Santa rashly.

"Me too, Santa?" asked Tommy Tucker.

"Everybody," promised Santa again. "Just come home now."

"Hurrah for Santa Claus!" shouted Jack Horner.

And in a moment they were all trooping back home, while the Pied Piper danced alone on Raspberry Road, never dreaming that they had forsaken him.

When the children all marched into Mrs. Claus's grown-up party, everybody was most surprised, and Mrs. Claus was really very much annoyed.

"Why in the world did you bring all the children of the town to my grown-up party, Santa?" she questioned him, "And where, pray, is the cow?"

But when all the parents had been told of what had happened that afternoon, they praised little Santa to the skies. They kissed him and blessed him and called him a good boy, until he thought he should die of embarrassment. And Mrs. Claus declared that, as reward, he should go to market with her to buy a fat pig the very next time she went.

At last, all the parents went home with their children held close to their sides, and the Claus family went to bed, tired and content. Just before he fell asleep, little Santa wondered how in the world he could ever make enough toys to go around among all the children of Pudding Lane. But, of course, a promise is a promise, and he had to do it somehow.

So that was really the way the young Santa got started on his annual custom of making Holy Day gifts for all the children he knew.

And how he loved to do it! He worked hours every day, and learned to make the most wonderful dolls, wooden animals, even rocking-horses whose tails were not stuck 'way over on one side.

That next Holy Day was the best Holy Day that Old King Cole's people ever had. And ever after that, Santa made toys for the Holy Day, and he became the most beloved person in the kingdom even though he was but a little boy, the son of a poor baker.

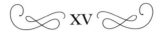

XV

A GREAT PROBLEM
IN THE CLAUS FAMILY

WHEN SANTA was almost a man, and had been making toys for years and years and years, the family gathered around the stove one day, to decide about Santa's future.

"He will be a baker and help me in the store," said Father Claus, who was longing for a good rest, anyway.

"He will be a carpenter," said Mother Claus. "He's too handy with his tools to be a baker, Mr. Claus."

"He will be a toy-maker," said the children.

At that Santa's face grew bright.

"Yes, I'd like to be a toy-maker," he said. "Matthew, Mark, Luke, and John can help you in the bakeshop, father. Only,—"

the boy stopped a moment,—"only, I shouldn't want to sell toys, you know."

"You shouldn't want to sell toys!" repeated Mrs. Claus. "Why, Santa Claus, whatever do you mean? Of course, you want to sell toys. No such toys were ever seen in the kingdom, and you will take in silver and gold by the bagful if you make them as a trade."

But young Santa was not pleased.

"I couldn't sell them, after giving them away all these years," he said.

At that Mrs. Claus lost her patience.

"And who, pray, is to pay for your lodging the rest of your life? Your poor father, who has worked so hard? Your brothers? Shame, Santa!"

Poor Santa Claus was very sorrowful.

"No, mother, no one is to pay for my lodging. But I must make toys to give away, I really must. I could never make them to sell."

The matter was left undecided, and everybody was very much worried. For here was Santa almost grown up, and there seemed to be no work for him to do. Santa himself was especially downcast, for he could not see, for the life of him, how he could ever make toys to give away and yet earn his lodging at the same time. And yet he felt inside himself that it would really be wrong for him to take money for his wonderful toys. And so it was perplexing problem.

Then one day, without any warning, Mother Goose swished down into their midst, with a great flourish of skirts, straight from the clouds on her trusty gander.

There was great rejoicing, for the lively old lady was much loved by her family, and her visits were far too few. She gave them all a hug, and when she got to Santa, she gave him an extra squeeze or so, for all the children he was her favorite.

"My goodness, Santa," she laughed. "I can't reach around you, you're so fat!"

Sure enough, her arms went only halfway round. For the fat little boy of years ago had become a big, round bellied fellow, with broad shoulders and wide girth, the jolliest-looking young chap you ever saw.

Then Mother Goose, whose eyes were as sharp as needles, noticed that there was a touch of sadness about the young man's face.

"Come, now, what's the matter?" she asked, but Santa did not answer, and as Mother Goose looked around the family, she saw that they all were distressed about something.

"Come, tell me immediately," she commanded.

So they told her what was troubling them. And after they had finished, Mother Goose sat silently thinking, thinking, thinking, for seven minutes. What *could* be done about her dear Santa and his strange desire to make toys and give them away to children the rest of his life?

At the end of the seven minutes, she looked up, and the whole family drew a breath of relief: for whenever Mother Goose put her mind on a difficulty, she always solved it.

"I have it," she announced. "Santa shall make toys for the children's Holy Day the rest of his life, and I myself will get Old King Cole to set him up in the business. Old King Cole has money-bags full of gold. It's time he did something handsome with it."

With that, Mother Goose got up from her chair, hopped on the gander, and in a moment was out of sight, almost before the family could catch their breath.

She had gone to see Old King Cole.

XVI

OLD KING COLE GIVES HIS ANSWER

THE FAMILY WAITED and waited for Mother Goose to return, fearful that she might fail in her errand, hopeful that she might succeed. They trembled as they waited; they hardly dared to move; nobody spoke. Santa himself felt that he should die if Mother Goose came back without the King's promise.

It seemed as if they had waited forever, when a flash of petticoats was seen through the window, and in three seconds Mother Goose was with them again. Her face was triumphant.

"The King says he will!" she cried. "It seems, Mr. Claus, that the King feels very much indebted to you for teaching the Queen to make tarts. She had always been such a restless woman. Well, well, Santa, there you are. What do you think of your old grandmother?"

The old lady laughed in delight at the good work she had done. Then she remembered something.

"Oh, I forgot to say there is one condition. The King says every child must be asleep on the night before Holy Day, or else, Santa, you cannot make their toys forever. But I guess they'll go to sleep, all right, if they want our Santa to make toys for them!"

The old lady laughed again, and then remembered something else.

"Oh, yes, here's the rest of it. You are to live, Santa Claus, in the great North Country, where the King has a big home and workshop, reindeer and sleighs galore."

At this, Santa's eyes almost popped out of his head, and the rest of the family just gasped. Mrs. Claus found her tongue first, as usual.

"In the North Country!" she exclaimed. "Why, Mother Goose, how ever will he get there?"

"Oh, he'll get there, all right," replied Mother Goose. "Old King Cole will see to that."

Such excitement as there was in Pudding Lane when it was learned that young Santa Claus was to be set up in the toy-making business by the King! How everybody gaped when it was told that he was to go far away to the North Country, to live in a big, big house, and ride behind reindeer galore.

The news flew from house to house like wildfire, until finally everyone but the Town Crier knew all about it. The Town

Crier was so busy calling out the price of butter that he didn't hear the story until his wife told him that evening. Then he hurried forth to ring the bell and cry the news. Nobody stopped him, for the Town Crier was getting a bit old and slow, and they were quite used to his calling out news that really wasn't news at all.

Everybody who lived in Pudding Lane came to see the Clauses, to ask questions, offer assistance, bring presents. Everybody loved Santa, you see and besides, the Clauses were Somebody, now that the King that taken them up.

It was all very pleasant and exciting, and everybody said that Santa was a very fortunate young man, and that Old King Cole was a merry old soul, was he.

Everybody was glad, it seemed, but the piper's wife, and she was jealous. For Tom, the piper's son, who ran away after he stole a pig, was the only person in Pudding Lane who had ever traveled any, and the piper's wife had taken on a good many airs about it for a long time. Now that Santa was going so far away, for such a noble career, she was very jealous. She found it hard to be even polite to the lucky Claus family.

XVII

SANTA GOES A-COURTING

FOR DAYS the Claus family worked hard to get Santa ready for this long journey to the North Country, where he was to live the rest of his life. Mrs. Claus made twelve red suits, each one a bit larger than the former one; for it was supposed that Santa would get just a little stouter each year. Mr. Claus baked many plum puddings and fruit cakes. The butcher brought over a ham. Mrs. Claus packed a boxful of flannels and goose oil and camphor against the freezing cold of the North.

And though they were all busy, they were just a little sad, too, to think of losing Santa. And Santa himself was depressed at the thought of going away so far. He knew he should be lonely, even in the midst of his beloved toy-making.

One day he was thinking of this, as he watched Mother Claus pack flannels into a box. All at once his mother looked up, and as if she had been reading his mind, spoke.

"Santa, it is not right for you to go to the North Country alone," she said.

"I shall be lonely," answered Santa.

"Then you must take a wife with you," said his mother decisively.

Young Santa stared.

"A wife," he said in amazement.

"A wife," repeated his mother. "Of course, you must have a wife. Whatever have we been thinking of not to get you a wife?"

Being a woman of action, Mrs. Claus left her packing, went into the bakeshop, and told Mr. Claus of her decision.

Mr. Claus agreed that Santa must have a wife. And so it was decided, though young Santa had not the faintest notion of how to get a wife.

"How *do* you get a wife?" he asked his father. It was really a very terrifying thought.

"You go out and court her," replied his father. "You take her sweets and posies. You make yourself agreeable to her and her family. You then get on your knees and say, 'Curly-locks, Curly-locks, will you be mine?' And if she's anything of a woman, she says she will. And that's all there is to it."

"But if her hair isn't curly?" objected Santa.

"All the better: she will be immensely flattered," answered Mr. Claus.

It sounded easy enough. But the next question was: who should the wife be?

"Jill is a nice girl," suggested Mr. Claus.

"Too clumsy," said Mother Claus.

"Always falling and sprawling around."

"Would Bo-Peep do?" asked Father Claus.

"Bo-Peep might do," answered his wife. "And yet she's always off somewhere hunting sheep. No, I hardly think she'd make a good practical wife."

Then Mrs. Claus thought of Bessie, the candlestick-maker's niece, who had just come to Pudding Lane. And Santa knew immediately that she was the very one.

Bessie was a lovely girl, with hair like streaming sun, and the most gleeful laugh in the whole world; and Santa had been admiring her as quite the nicest girl he knew. He was sure that she would make an excellent wife, and that, with her in the North Country, he would never be lonely.

So that evening, he went a-courting. He took posies and sweets, he made himself very agreeable, and he said: "Curly-locks, Curly-locks, will you be mine?"

He did not get on his knees, being a bit stout for that, but he made a deep bow, for his mother said that would do very well for a fat fellow.

Bessie said she would be happy to become Mrs. Santa Claus. Santa rushed home to tell his glorious news.

"Bless us all!" said Mrs. Claus.

"Great snakes!" said Mr. Claus.

Then they all went to bed.

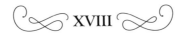

XVIII

THE WEDDING AND THE
WEDDING JOURNEY

THE WEDDING was held in the bakeshop, at noon on the following Monday. Pudding Lane had never seen such a grand occasion.

Everybody was there, even the King and Queen. The fiddlers three played the music. Mistress Mary supplied the flowers from her garden. There was a great feast of tarts, which the Queen of Hearts made from her own royal hands. Everybody had on new clothes. Santa's sister, now a big girl, wore the kid slippers that had pinched her mother's feet at that other party so long ago.

Only Mrs. Solomon Grundy was not in holiday mood. She, poor woman, kept referring to her own unfortunate marriage. But then everybody was used to Mrs. Grundy, so nobody really listened to her as she mumbled: "Married on Wednesday, ill on Thursday," and so on.

And after all the celebration and feasting, the Happy Couple, as the Town Crier called them, rode off in a golden chariot, lent by the King. Mother Claus cried a few tears; Father Claus sniffed a bit; the candlestick-maker went back to his bench, croaking and shaking his head.

But, in the golden chariot, Mrs. And Mrs. Santa Claus were as happy as birds.

They rode along Raspberry Road, turned at Pinafore Pike, went through Hamelin and Banbury Cross, and finally they came to the edge of the North Country, where it was beginning to be cold. Into the North Woods went the golden chariot, and every hour it grew colder and colder.

At last they came to open country, where deep thick snow lay on the ground. There they were met by a sleigh and eight reindeer, whole bells jingled a noisy, sweet welcome to them. Into the sleigh they jumped, and then they were off, slipping across the snow like a flash of light, until they came to the great house where they were to live.

What a wonderful house it was—a great, wide, low building, furnished with log furniture, and bear skins, and with a fire blazing in every room. Mrs. Santa Claus cried aloud when she saw it, and Santa himself stamped around saying, "Ho, ho, ho!" and rubbing his hands with pleasure.

It was surely the best place in the world to live, they thought. But the next day they buckled right down to business, for, of course, there were heaps and heaps of toys to be made, and Santa was most anxious to get everything done in good time.

XIX

THE FIRST CHRISTMAS

ALL YEAR LONG Mr. and Mrs. Santa Claus worked to make toys.

Santa cut down straight pines and spruce trees. He carved dolls and horses and rabbits out of the wood, and Mrs. Claus painted them until her arms ached. He made dolls of sawdust and linen, and Mrs. Claus dressed them in the latest doll styles, in blue and pink silk, with laces on the edge of their bonnets. Santa made a roomful of rocking-horses—it seemed that every little boy in the world wanted a rocking-horse. And Mrs. Santa made candy until she said she thought she'd turn into candy. Whereupon Santa told her she was sweet enough for that, anyway!

And then, on Christmas Eve, he started out, bundled to the chin in fur robes. The sleigh was running over with toys. He carried his pockets full, too, and under his arm was a bundle of dolls that just would not squeeze in any place else.

"And will you hurry back, Santa Claus?" asked his wife anxiously, just before he started.

"If all the children are abed and asleep as they should be, I'll be back by the crack of dawn," he promised.

"And if some little boy or girl is awake?" questioned Mrs. Claus fearfully.

"Well"—Santa sighed deeply at the thought of such a calamity. "Well, I should simply have to bring all the toys home, and we could never try the business again. For Old King Cole explicitly said that every child must be sound asleep on the eve before Holy Day, or we'd have to go back to Pudding Lane and be bakers the rest of our lives."

Then he was off, with a snap and a flourish, and Mrs. Claus went back into the house, to sit by the fire and wait.

The clock ticked, ticked, ticked. The snow outside fell softly, softly, softly. The fire burned lower, lower, lower. And Mrs. Claus's heart almost stood still, so fearful was she that some boy or girl would be awake and spoil Santa's visit.

Supposing, she thought to herself, supposing little Polly Flinders had sat up to warm her toes in the cinders, as she was so fond of doing? Oh, dear! Poor Mrs. Claus almost wept at the very thought.

Or supposing that Greedy Nan insisted on staying up, as she always, always did when Sleepy-head suggested Bed?

Or supposing some little boy hid behind a sofa and peeped!

Mrs. Santa could hardly bear these thoughts. She got up and paced the floor in her anxiety. And when she did that, even Santa's cat, who had been snoozing gently by the wood-box, became restless. He followed Mrs. Claus up and down the room as she walked back and forth. He wondered where his master was, and what was the matter with Mrs. Claus. He had a worried frown between his green eyes, and his whiskers drooped dolefully.

It was almost the crack of dawn. Mrs. Claus strained her ears for the faraway sound of sleigh-bells, and peered out of the window for the first sight of a sleigh. But she heard no sound, and saw nothing in the distance. Oh, she was so afraid they would have to give up the toy-making business and go back to Pudding Lane!

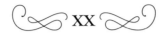

SANTA COMES HOME

BUT JUST as that moment dawn cracked. A dim light shone in the east. The snowbirds began to chirp. The stars faded softly out.

And then, in a rush of snow and with a clamor of bells, came Santa, driving the reindeer with one hand, and waving to Mrs. Claus with the other; laughing aloud, "Ho, ho, ho!" In a second he was in the house, stamping and chuckling, puffing like a great steam-engine.

"It's all right, Mrs. Santa, it's all right!" he shouted. "Every child was sound asleep, and we can go on forever now."

At this wonderful news, Mrs. Santa cried a bit, then set to work getting Santa's breakfast.

The cat, hearing all that all was well again, grinned broadly and climbed up in Santa's lap. Santa sat by the fire, stroking him and chuckling aloud.

And so it is that Santa Claus has come every year since that first Christmas, and will keep on coming—forever.

THE END

SARAH ADDINGTON
American Author (1891 – 1940)

Following her graduation from Earlham College, Sarah Addington attended Columbia University where she graduated as the only female member of the first class of the Pulitzer School of Journalism. In 1915 she became a writer for the Sunday magazine section of the *New York Tribune*. She became the assistant publicity director of the National American Women Suffrage Association and was working for the organization in 1917 when the state of New York granted the vote to women. She married in 1917 but continued to write under her maiden name. From 1921 to 1923 Sarah Addington was on the staff of the popular magazine *The Ladies' Home Journal. The Boy Who Lived in Pudding Lane*, Sarah's charming story of Santa Claus as a young boy first appeared in print in the December 1921 issue of the magazine and was released in hardcover in 1922.

GERTRUDE A. KAY
American illustrator (1884-1939)

Gertrude Kay studied illustration at the Philadelphia Museum School of Design and with Howard Pyle at the Drexel Institute in Philadelphia. She produced covers and story illustrations for *Ladies' Home Journal* and other magazines from around 1908 through the 1920s. She is well known as an illustrator of children's books, including a popular 1923 edition of *Alice In Wonderland*.

Santa, driving the reindeer with one hand, and waving to Mrs. Claus with the other

Published in the USA and in Canada in 2017 by GRAFTON & SCRATCH PUBLISHERS
www.graftonandscratch.com
Distributed by Atlas Books/Bookmasters Ohio, USA

Book design by Elisa Gutiérrez

The text is set in Goudy Old Style, first released in 1915 and designed by American
typographer and book designer Frederic W. Goudy. Titles and ornaments are
from the typeface Fantasy by Sabrina Mariela Lopez, published by Typesenses.

Printed in the US   10 9 8 7 6 5 4 3 2 1

LIBRARY AND ARCHIVES CANADA CATALOGUING IN PUBLICATION

Addington, Sarah, 1891-1940, author
     The boy who lived in Pudding Lane : being a true account, if
only you believe it, of the life and ways of Santa, oldest son of Mr.
and Mrs. Claus / Sarah Addington ; illustrated by Gertrude A. Kay.

Originally published in 1922.
Issued in print and electronic formats.

ISBN 978-1-927979-26-6 (hardcover).~ISBN 978-1-927979-27-3 (HTML).~

ISBN 978-1-927979-28-0 (PDF)

     I. Kay, Gertrude A. (Gertrude Alice), 1884-1939, illustrator II. Title.

PZ8.A224Bo 2017   j813'.52   C2017-901592-3
                                                              C2017-901593-1